AF414531

Summary

Jax

I don't need a reason to go on vacation with my best friend, Sierra, but I've got several. One of them being my impending wedding, and my desire to be far, far away from the groom. This vacation is all about girl time and "me time," so the last thing I need is to meet and fall for a soft-spoken resort employee. But, the refreshingly shy, polite and slightly nerdy Brooks is unlike anyone I've ever met. The more I see him, the faster his shyness burns off like fog in the South Pacific sunshine, and soon the life I left behind is a distant memory.

Brooks

I meet a lot of celebrities on this rock, and none of them have ever left me starstruck. Until the day Jax Pierce walks into my life. As a man with no game when it comes to women, I'm not prepared for this day. More importantly, all I can think about is my lifelong crush on this woman. I feel as awkward as I felt at 13, and it shows in the way I keep tripping over my words and missing her jokes. However, the more time I spend with Jax, the more I realize what she needs. Me. I might not have moves, but I do have enthusiasm, loyalty, and complete devotion. There's no choice in the matter; she's going to be on an island vacation with me for the rest of our lives.

Chapter One

Brooks

ONLY ONE HUMAN in this world would feel unlucky about accidentally grabbing the perfect ass of Jax Pierce. That's me, Dr. Brooks Barrow. I'm that human. That very awkward human who has no business being anywhere in the vicinity of this woman and her notably coveted backside.

Oh sure, it's plump and round and utterly squeezable, like a nice cool pillow on a hot summer night.

Her famously beautiful rump is just as I'd imagined it would be.

The problem is that Jax didn't consent to the grabbing. She doesn't even know my name.

Some men would kill to be in my shoes right now. Me? This is not how I had planned to introduce myself if ever given a chance to meet my lifelong celebrity crush.

Celebrity might be a strong word. To most people,

she's just a model, a social media influencer, an actor in commercials.

To me, Jax is a legend, featuring heavily in my first ever wet dream at the age of 13 and at least weekly ever since then. She's also a client at Cerulean Resort, and I'm supposed to be her kayak guide to Temple Island for a morning donkey yoga class.

So how did I end up groping her peach?

That would be a direct result of me not paying attention to the local wildlife. What happened was, Jax became very excited at the sight of a fin breaching the water less than twenty feet away as we paddled toward Temple Island.

"Dolphin!"

I'm such a know-it-all. I couldn't help myself. I'm the naturalist around here; it's my job to know these things.

"That's a basking shark."

Gasping and freaking out a bit, Jax began paddling away like mad. As we were still in shallow water, her oar hit the bottom with extra force, and the vessel capsized. Me, I kayak every day, and I know how to extract myself underwater safely. Jax had informed me this was her first time in such a watercraft. So, thinking quickly, I dove for her.

In the heat of a newfound irrational rush of protective instinct, I hadn't realized the kayak had already dumped her out entirely, and her life vest was fully functional, and so were her legs. And we were in waist-deep, utterly clear water. Jax was in no danger other than the danger of being molested by me. What I thought was her middle turned out to be her rump.

And that's where I currently find myself. Inappropriately touching, but, as a consummate naturalist, needing to be sure we don't startle the shark or, most likely, step on a stingray. "Don't move," I say. "Basking sharks won't bother you, but let's try to be still, and maybe it'll come closer, and we can get a good look at that huge mouth."

She squeaks, a sound of an anxious little kitten. I desperately want her to be calm and know that nothing will happen to her. I'm the guy everyone turns to for animal facts on this island; I know what I'm doing.

"It's gone now. Off to look for plankton elsewhere."

"Hopefully, they can't smell white-hot fear," she mutters.

"Unless you're made of plankton, you're safe. And if you are made of plankton, you're much too big of a conquest for a juvenile of that size," I say.

I say this without thinking. Bugs and animals and trees? I know all the things. Women? I know nothing.

"Excuse me?" Jax swivels around to face me, then gives me a strange look, and I realize my hands are still on her. Granted, no longer gripping her bottom but firmly on her waist.

And then I realize what I just said. "I just meant ounce for ounce, you'd be a daunting meal."

She arches an eyebrow at me. "Really?"

Even though this early morning water is so cold my nuts are retreating into my body cavity, my pits are sweating like July on the equator.

"You see," I say, instinctively pushing up my prescription sunglasses on the bridge of my nose. "Humans in general are…."

"Relax, Dr. Jones. I'm fucking with you."

"Oh," I say, confused.

It's then I notice she's smiling. "Well, not about being freaked out about the shark. That was genuine terror. But thank you for…saving my ass."

Her eyes drop down and back up to meet my gaze. Yes,

I'm still holding on to her even though she's fine. Completely fine.

I let go. "I'm not Dr. Jones. I'm Dr. Barrow. But you don't have to call me doctor; you can call me Brooks."

She has the most lovely laugh. "Once again, I'm fucking with you."

My mind races, and finally, I see what she did.

"Oh, Indiana Jones. Now I get it. You're funny," I say sincerely.

Her already bright, cheerful face somehow becomes even more brilliant. She could outshine a full moon on a cloudless night. I knew from her internet channel that she was gorgeous and hilarious. In person, she's breathtaking.

"Thank you," she says.

Awkwardly, I find myself staring at her until I remember that I'm soaked to the skin in my rash guard shirt and Bermuda shorts. I look like a drowned rat. She, with her long, wet hair held together on top of her head, looks ready for yoga. Wet yoga.

That's not supposed to be sexy, Brooks. Just observing she's wet is not supposed to turn you on. You work on an island in the South Pacific. If you're going to think horny thoughts every time someone falls into the water, you're going to get yourself into trouble.

Already way ahead of us, her friend in the other kayak calls out to us. I inwardly cringe, realizing her companion has witnessed this awkward moment in living color. "You guys coming?"

"Well, we'd better be on our way to yoga," Jax says.

"Do you need to go back to the dock and grab some dry yoga pants?"

She shakes her head and smirks at me. "I'm good. I'm going to get sweaty anyway, might as well get a head start."

I should be used to her double entendres; I've been watching her channel for years. She could talk about health insurance and make a joke about her pussy. I know more about her genitalia than anyone should know.

But my cock is still thinking like a thirteen-year-old boy, waking up with wet *Star Wars* sheets after staying up too late watching a teenage Jax romp around in her workout videos. I feel equally ashamed of myself too. She's always been a woman to me, deserving of respect. Yet, animal attraction is animal attraction.

Her gaze dips down to my chest and back up to my eyes. I let go of her and feel myself turn beet red. God, I hope she doesn't register a complaint with my boss for grabbing her.

We arrive at Temple Island without further incident, and I enjoy a hike around the grounds perimeter while the instructor guides her and her friend and a handful of others through a sun salutation. I've never done yoga; I've never felt coordinated enough for that. My legs are stumpy, and my arms are too bulky to pretzel on a mat.

The truth is, I shouldn't even be here. It was by pure luck that I met Jax today. The usual guide in charge of water sports is ill this morning (more likely nursing a hang-over—we all saw him stumbling off with one of the other female guests for whom he was buying drinks at the Mumbling Ahab last night).

If Baker had been here? I would have missed my chance to meet Jax because there's no way this guest would be booking the kind of outings I conduct for the resort. Got a question about bugs, birds, and poisonous mush-rooms? I'm your guy. Want to learn how to dive off a cliff? Better call Baker.

As I make my way down the empty beach, I look out from the white sand and across the turquoise waters. Off in the distance, I notice what we islanders call a "white boat," a yacht anchored in the water, about half a mile offshore.

Odd place to drop anchor, as the open sea can get 12-foot swells. Most yacht captains prefer to stick to the water within the crescent of islands that make up this country. But who knows why these one-percenters do what they do.

One thing about working on a private island is we see a lot of celebrities make bad decisions.

Up until today, meeting a famous person never rattled me. Jax is the only famous person I give a shit about. And I'm still shook.

"Get your head in the game, Brooks," I tell myself. I then recall there's a whole colony of sea turtle eggs on the west side of the island, so I head that way, checking my watch to make sure I have time. I spend the rest of the ninety-minute class shoring up the barricades around the nests on the beach and checking the area to make sure guests are obeying the signage. It's usually not a problem since Temple Island is only used for day outings. There are no bars or hotels here, just pristine beaches, a donkey sanctuary, some dense forest, and a flat stone surface that marks the ruins of an ancient temple, where now people pay hundreds of extra dollars to do yoga next to some sweet, curious donkeys.

When the yoga class ends, Jax turns and sees me waiting by her kayak.

She runs up to me, and I ask how the class went.

"I feel amazing, Dr. Jones," she says with a deep, contented sigh and a stretch, a blissed-out look on her face.

That's because you are, generally speaking, amazing, Jax Pierce.

And that's the moment when I know I'm going to break the number one rule of Cerulean Resort: Don't fraternize with the guests, especially not the celebrities.

Chapter Two

Jax

I WISH I would have paid attention to Shark Week on
television. If I had, I would have been able to identify that
fin poking out of the water, and I would not have caused a
scene in full view of everyone at the boathouse.

I point and squeal, "Look! A dolphin!"

My guide, the cute but nerdy guy from the resort, tells
me right away the thing I don't want to hear. "No, that's a
basking shark."

I twist around a little too abruptly and shriek, "What?!"

As I turn, the kayak goes off balance and flips,
dumping both me and the kayak guide into the water, with
the shark.

Not only is this my first time being in the water near a
shark in the open sea, but it's also my first time in a kayak.
Let me just say there's nothing that makes me feel quite
like trapped shark bait as a long plastic vessel in which I
can't move my legs. I might as well be stuffed inside a

human-sized Kong toy, but for marine predators. Well, I got myself into this mess, and I'm going to get us out of this water, or else I'm going to be lunch.

"It's okay, don't panic," says the supposed shark expert.

Excellent advice. Wonder if he's got any practical advice in his repertoire for someone already panicking.

I don't necessarily need a man to save me, but my kayak guide doesn't see things that way.

Specifically, he seems to think holding on to my butt is the way to keep me calm. I mean, he's not wrong. He does have big, strong hands.

It seems to me he grabbed me there by accident and now doesn't seem able to let go. Is this sexual harassment or something else? Feels like something else. Is this flustered, shy fellow fun to watch as he fumbles over his words? Absolutely.

Am I also finding him adorable? Yes.

Have I been sheltered from dating men so long that I'm secretly curious if this bashful nerd is a freak in the bedroom? Also yes.

God, Jax. If this person knew what you were thinking about right now, he would probably run and hide and never speak to you again.

Eventually, I make it to donkey yoga class, which turns out to be the best activity I could have chosen to kick off the first full day of vacation — or my would-be honeymoon, depending on whom you ask.

When I return to the kayak to find Brooks there waiting for me, I feel another round of butterflies. And, I feel bad for giving shit to this man, who has introduced himself as a doctor. He's due a little more respect than being labeled a nerd.

"Thanks for rescuing my butt," I say.

"You would have been fine," he replies, helping me don

my life preserver. "Humans are in less danger around sharks than they are at, say, a random bar on vacation on a remote island."

I'm taken aback by this comment. "I get nature lessons and self-defense advice. Was that part of the package?"

Brooks seems to take everything I say at face value and does not recognize the sarcasm.

"Well, this isn't my job. The water sports director pulled me in to escort you because he was tied up elsewhere. But if you are interested in nature, I am doing a volcano tour later."

We begin to paddle our way back to the main resort, and I make a mental note of how easily we fall into sync with our oars. Especially now that I'm less nervous, knowing I have a wildlife expert as my escort.

"Am I going to fall into hot lava? Because if there's lava, I will be the first to fall into it. As you can see, I'm not as graceful as people assume," I say as I consider his proposal.

Brooks answers in a deep, authoritative voice. "The volcano is dormant; you're perfectly safe with me."

Why does this reply produce an odd sensation of flames licking my thighs and butterflies fluttering in my stomach?

He presses on, "And if you enjoy the volcano tour, then you should sign up for my jungle foraging tour."

I snort. "I hate bugs even more than I hate lava. Especially the dragonflies that are so big they could eat me."

And this is where I put my foot in my mouth because he replies, "Bugs are my life. They're the reason I became a biologist."

"Oh. Sorry."

"No worries. But dragonflies are the best. They don't bite, and they eat mosquitoes."

Warming up to the idea, I tell him, "Sign me up for the volcano, and we'll see where that goes, Doctor."

"Okay, I will," Brooks says, sounding very pleased with himself. "It might not be as exciting as cliff diving, but you'll be glad you did it. Very 'Gram-worthy."

Surprised he has any thoughts about Instagram, I awkwardly, carefully, pivot in my seat to get a look at him. Is he a follower of mine? In his wide-brimmed outdoor hat, polarized goggles, Teva sandals, and khaki uniform, Brooks is not like anyone in my world.

I doubt he's a follower. If I had to guess when I met this man a little bit ago, I'd say he doesn't have time for social media. He looks exactly like the kind of guy who spends all day plucking trash out of the ocean and helping beached whales find their pods again. A bigger, quieter, and less intense Steve Irwin. Now, that's a nature show I would watch.

Chapter Three

Brooks

"This is Beth. Do you copy?"

The radio clipped to my hip chirps with the sound of the hotel concierge. I ignore it at first.

I'm in the middle of explaining to some guests on the beach that the islands have banned the ingredients in their sunscreen due to its bleaching effect on the local coral reefs. "But I burn so easily," complains this woman, who is about thirty seconds away from a fine if she doesn't stop slathering her children with parabens.

"Brooks, it's Beth. Do you copy?"

I simply hand over a complimentary bottle of approved sunscreen and take away the other stuff, slipping it into my pocket while I walk away, ignoring the family's outrage at my blatant theft. I don't care. I'd take it away whether I was paid to behave this way or not.

Grudgingly I answer. "This is Brooks. Go." Trudging

around the protected dune, I find a shady palm tree and listen to Beth.

"Have you been checking your Google docs?"

I told the previous concierge to radio me when a guest expressed interest in one of my guided nature outings. I keep a handwritten chart in my wallet. This new one, Beth, insists on using Google docs.

"My phone is for emergencies," I say. "That's all I use it for." That, and also for watching Jax Pierce gallivant around her bedroom and backyard, giving makeup, hair, fitness, and style tutorials.

Beth grumbles something. "Fine. Can you come to the lobby and look at this, please?"

"On my way," I mutter on the way back to the hotel from the beach. Being indoors is like a punishment for me. Using technology to keep a schedule, even more so.

Beth shoots me a look of exasperation when I trudge over to her mahogany desk in the open-air lobby, next to an enormous glass urn full of fruit water. On my way over, I go out of my way to switch off the lamps in the lobby that no one is using at the moment. Beth stands aside and gestures for me to take a look at her computer screen.

What I see there might be even better than an all-night binge of Jax Pierce's YouTube channel. Every single one of my nature excursions has been booked for the next two weeks. And the name of the guest who signed up? Jax Pierce. On every single line.

I feel an urge to thump my chest and announce I'm the king of the jungle. *Hell yes.* The day after tomorrow, I'm taking my childhood crush on a hike in the wilderness. Alone.

And that's just the beginning.

Is this what it feels like to be one of the cool guys in school? That's child's play.

This is what it felt like at man's discovery of fire.

Chapter Four

Jax

"What's a naturalist?" Sierra asks, sipping her mango juice over breakfast.

She's looking radiant and relaxed after yesterday's massage and nap on the beach. I'm sure it has nothing to do with her run-in with that sexy pilot Austin.

Today we're hiking the volcano crater, so we're taking full advantage of the breakfast buffet to build up our strength.

I've just been telling her about my conversation with the kayak guide and that I've signed up for every stinking excursion the guy offers for resort guests.

I have to think about Sierra's question because I didn't ask Brooks. "I don't know. Like a park ranger, I guess? Well, a park ranger who can't arrest people."

Sierra takes a bite of her toast. "Park rangers already cannot arrest people," she snorts.

"Oh yes, they can. Remember my 19th birthday party?"

Sierra scrunches up her face in thought. If only I were kidding. Leave it to my father's business associates to cause such a scene at a ski lodge that the forestry authorities showed up and asked them to leave. It was supposed to be a low-key trip with just a few of my friends, but it had turned into … something else. My father and the people who finance his record label are loud, overbearing, and obnoxious.

"I hope our pilot stud friend appreciates that chipmunk face of yours."

Sierra blushes and shoots me a look just as my phone rings. I check the screen and promptly ignore it.

"Was that Louis?" Sierra asks, looking a little freaked.

No. Worse than my would-be fiancé. I shake my head. "My dad's security guy, Damian."

"Are you going to answer?"

"Not today. Not while I'm on vacation."

"Sooner or later, you're going to have to tell your dad where you are."

I blink and glance down at the screen where I see he's left a voicemail.

"Then my father should call me himself instead of passing it off to his flunky," I say.

Chapter Five

Brooks

I KNEW I should not have let Jax's interest in my activities put thoughts into my head. I knew I would let it tell me stories that aren't real.

All morning I've been preening like a peacock in the mirror, combing my hair, and practicing charming things to say to Jax. I let myself get carried away on the idea that her signing up for two weeks' worth of hikes and adventures meant she was into me.

But upon arrival at the tour, I learn it was all too good to be true. She's here with her friend Sierra and Austin Fisher, the ruggedly handsome bush pilot. Of course, she'd be interested in the pilot. He's got that quiet, broody side that women like. He's a man of action. Austin has game coming out of his ears.

Sure, I can identify the genus and species of any exotic bird in this jungle, but I can't talk about beer or sports or whatever other dudes talk about. I certainly can't captivate a girl with stories about dangerous fighter jet missions around the world. I'm a geek in cargo shorts and a pith helmet, administering organic bug spray to resort guests.

As if to illustrate that point, Austin saves the day when the worst possible thing that could happen on one of my tours happens. A child, who has been falling behind the tour group because he's become distracted by the wildlife, tumbles off the trail and falls down the slope of the crater. Not minutes after I've told him not to sit on the back of a tortoise. The little shit.

Everyone panics, except Austin. In superhero fashion, he uses a vine to rappel down to where the kid is barely hanging on. I mean, the scene could be straight out of a movie, and he might as well have been using a whip to pull him and the kid up. Who's Dr. Jones now?

I manage to inch myself down the rocky slope far enough to help Austin hand the kid off to me. I forget all about Jax for a minute while I'm making sure the kid is all right and not injured. After I make arrangements for Isaac and his parents to have the golf carts meet them at the rim of the crater, I fully expect the woman in my dreams to be fawning all over the guy.

But Jax surprises me once again.

"I'll go with you to the rim to see them off," she says.

I look from her to her friend and Austin, and I'm confused. "You don't have to…."

Jax unexpectedly slides her arm through mine. "You look a little shaken."

What is happening? Why is she doing this instead of finishing the hike with her friend?

"I didn't think you'd want to miss out on the hot spring. Some people say it's the best part of the tour," I stammer, feeling anxiety sweat at her touch, on top of the usual layer of tropics sweat. I'm anxious not because I don't want her to touch me but because I know how this goes. One false move on my part, one misinterpreted flirtation, and I'm out in the cold.

She replies, "The best part of the tour was watching you save that kid."

"Austin did most of the work," I say.

Jax laughs as we make our way down the side of the mountain, following the golf cart carrying the kid's family.

"You should learn how to take a compliment," she says.

Thoughtlessly, I say, "You must be very used to compliments."

"Why, because I'm a model?"

"No, because you're angelically beautiful."

Chapter Six

Jax

PEOPLE all my life told me I was pretty. When I grew up, they said I was "hot."

Nobody ever said "angelically beautiful."

As soon as we drop Isaac and his family back at the villas, I can tell Brooks wants to ask me something. For starters, he cuts the motor of our little electric golf cart. The sudden silence enhances the crashing of waves, the sea bird calls, the sounds of complete relaxation. I lower my shoulders, remembering what yesterday's yoga instructor kept telling me.

"May I treat you to lunch?"

I blink at him. "You do know my lunches are included in the resort package."

"Oh. Right. Sorry."

Oh, no. Does he think I just turned him down?

But then his face breaks into a shy smile as he rests his sunglasses on top of his head. "Please tell me you're fucking with me again because offering food is about all I know how to do around a beautiful woman."

I shouldn't fuck with my new nerd friend. But he's so adorable when he's flustered; I can't resist fucking with him.

"Sure," I tell him. "I could emotionally stuff my face with something after nearly watching that kid plummet to his death."

His gaze leaves mine like he's thinking of a place to go.

"I know the perfect place for emotional face stuffing, but it's just outside the resort. I know it well."

If I didn't know any better, I'd say Brooks was trying to be charming.

"I thought Cerulean owned the entire island."

He nods. "It does. We have to go by boat to one of the keys."

"As long as you don't grab my ass again," I tease.

He blanches. "I'm so sorry about that. And I'm doing the paddling."

This is too easy. "No paddling me, either."

The poor man is now the same shade of red that my lobster was at dinner last night.

"Kidding!"

He groans.

"Stop worrying about all that. You have a good grip," I say with a smirk.

Brooks's expression moves from flustered to hungry before he catches himself. The change happens around his eyes, like someone in a vampire movie. It's just a dim flash of need like he forgot all about his embarrassment at my teasing and wants to eat me. And then the look disappears like he's working hard to get control of his emotions.

He starts the motor once again, and we're off.

My phone rings, startling me out of getting lost in

Brooks's eyes. The name that appears on the screen: "Damian." My knee-jerk reaction is to silence it, drop it in my pocket, and fidget with my hands.

"I don't mind if you need to take a call. You don't need to feel like this is a date."

"It's not?"

"Ah, well, I mean. Do you want it to be a date?"

"What do you want this to be, Brooks?"

He's quiet until we arrive at a remote dock on the island's south end, tucked away in a cove surrounded by dense trees. Here, he helps me into a small sailboat. Thank god, the water is calm today. And, thank god, no more kayaks.

He doesn't answer my question until he's rowed us well offshore.

"No one has ever asked me what I want. I don't particularly enjoy dating. It's difficult. I don't know how to flirt. What I want is to spend time with you, and that's all I know."

My body stills as my fingers grip the weathered wooden bench at the approach of a slight swell in the water, rocking the sailboat gently. I breathe it all in, every word he just said.

I don't want to dump too much information on him, but the truth is, he has no idea what that means to me. My entire life has been in the presence of people who want things from me, not people who simply want to spend time with me. Sierra has always been the only exception to that. And now, there's Brooks.

"Lunch" turns out to be an impromptu al fresco picnic on a tiny, untouched beach on the opposite side of the smallest island in The Pearl Crescent. Sitting here on a piece of driftwood while Brooks expertly chops open a coconut in the groove of a palm tree, while looking out onto the open sea, away from the view of the other islands on the horizon, feels like we're stranded together on a deserted island.

"You're the person I would take with me," I say.

He splits open the coconut and offers me a drink after showing me how to drink it straight out of the fruit.

"What person?" Brooks asks.

I take a drink, and though coconut water has never been my favorite, this is so much better than I thought it would be. "The person I'd take if I were allowed to choose five things to take to a desert island to survive. You'd be the one to find food and build a raft."

He shrugs and begins wandering into the trees again. I get the feeling we're not headed to a restaurant for lunch, but we're going to live off the land instead for the next hour, or two, or three. All of that sounds perfect to me. "Eh, most people could find it in themselves to find food and shelter, even build a raft."

Snorting, I respond that I would be the one to capsize the raft and ruin everyone's rescue.

He laughs. "Then I guess we'd be stuck here together for the rest of our lives. I can think of worse punishments."

God, he's so corny. So corny, I would not think twice about sitting on his face to keep him quiet.

"What else would you bring to your desert island?"

I need more information. "How many items do I get?"

Brooks has been climbing trees, cutting down fruit. Now, he's retrieved a stash of fishing poles and has me standing in the water because I suppose we're going to catch our lunch now.

"Hmm," he says, thinking. "Five things in addition to your choice of a person."

"Besides you? I'd bring my playlist that Sierra made for my sweet sixteen."

"That assumes you'd be bringing something to play it on," Brooks says.

"Well, then I'd have to bring my phone. And my Bluetooth speaker," I add.

"Presumably, we'd have nothing to play it on as there would be nowhere to charge your phone."

I raise a finger into the air. "Aha! I'm also bringing a solar-powered charger."

"Fair enough. One more item."

I answer instantly. "My USB rechargeable vibrator."

All is quiet for several moments. I stare into the water and pray for a fish to swim along and take the bait. I thought with Brooks being a naturalist; he wouldn't be embarrassed by the topic of human biological needs.

He clears his throat, and I no longer am praying for a fish on the hook. I wish for the Kraken to surface and swallow me whole.

Chapter Seven

Brooks

ALL RATIONAL THOUGHT has left the building. My brain has transitioned into horny degenerate territory, and it may never recover.

Bugs? Birds? Animal facts? All gone. In their place is my imagination's picture of the beautiful Jax, spread-eagle on a raft, naked from the waist down, pleasuring herself with…what? I don't even know. She freely talks about devices from time to time on her YouTube channel, but I never know what she's talking about.

All I know for sure is whatever she's thinking about inserting into her vee on this hypothetical desert island is going to have to get out of the way to make room for daddy.

Did I just call myself "daddy"? Yuck. What's happening to me?

"Moving right along," I say, which is me stalling for time.

"Did I embarrass you, Brooks?"

"Me? Embarrassed? No, why would you think that?"

"Because you said nothing for a very long time."

I clear my throat. "I was thinking about…thinking about my list."

"You tell me your favorite sex toy, and I'll tell you mine."

"*Avatar.*"

What? "Is that what you named your fleshlight? Is the pussy part, like, blue or something?"

"The movie I would take to the desert island. *Avatar.*"

She laughs at her mistake. "Once again, assuming you have something to watch it on."

I turn to her, and once again, I feel a flash of that hunger. This time, I don't bother hiding it.

Jax turns away and drinks from her water bottle. While her eyes leave mine, I can't help but see the way her lips turn a darker shade of pink. I'd like to find out if what they say is true about nipples matching the lips. For science. But not here…not on our first date.

"Well, if we're together on this island, then you have a phone and a charger, so we're all set, aren't we?"

Jax smiles shyly. She's not shy as a rule, but I'm sure my awkwardness makes her uncomfortable. My pulse races. My throat feels dry. This whole conversation was meant to be lighthearted, but now there seems to be a lot more going on under the surface.

"Right. We're together," she rasps.

"So I've got you, my favorite movie. And after that, I suppose I'd have my copy of *Origin of Species.*"

Jax pretends to snore. "I'm sorry, what book?"

"It's got all my notes in the margins. I've had it since I was 11 years old," I say, chuckling. I know; I've gotten shit over my preferred reading material my entire life.

"All right, I guess I'll have to write my own erotica. What else?"

I'm quiet for another moment, then I say, "A machete for clearing brush and cutting bamboo to make a shelter. And my Bowie knife for hunting and making spears for fishing. And that's it."

"You've got two more items, plus a person, Doctor."

"That's all I need as long as I have you."

I enjoy watching her face react in surprise. Her eyebrows go up, and she's speechless. For a few seconds, anyway. And then, she licks her lips; my cock twitches.

"Because I'm the one with the charger and the phone," Jax says. "I feel overpacked in comparison."

Finally, our protein arrives in the form of an unsuspecting grouper. Minutes later, the two of us are stuffing our faces with a feast of fruit, fish, and crab over a campfire.

"As restaurants go, this one gets a five-star review from me on Yelp," she comments.

I'm glad she's happy, but my lizard brain is still thinking about that vibrator.

Her phone rings again, disquieting our little zen moment.

Again, she's not answering it.

My mood is starting to shift into overprotective. I'm curious about who's bothering her and how I can make them go away. "Are you going to tell me who that is so I can put a stop to it?"

She looks at me, a bit surprised at my tone.

"It's my father. Well, no. Damian is my father's personal hired gun who likes to think he's my bodyguard. I'm…well…I suppose now is a good time to tell you. This vacation was supposed to be my honeymoon."

My stomach falls into my feet. "You're married?"

Jax shakes her head. "No! God, no. I ran away."

Relieved but still on a roller coaster, I can't help but find this a bit amusing. "You left some poor sap at the altar?"

Jax squares her lovely shoulders and fixes me with a determined stare. "Listen. He's no poor sap. Louie will be fine; he doesn't love me. And I can't stand him."

Geez. I thought I knew everything about this girl from obsessively, secretly following every move she makes online. But it turns out I know nothing. "Then why would you get engaged?"

Jax scoffs haughtily. "I didn't get engaged. Not voluntarily. It was all arranged by my father."

I look around the island. "Excuse me, but it's the 2020s, and you are an adult American. That's not a thing."

Once again, her look bores through me. "It's a thing if your father fancies himself a successful music producer and borrows money from bad people to finance his lavish lifestyle."

I don't follow, and I tell her as much.

"Be right back," she says, getting up to wash her hands and face in the water after finishing our meal. When she returns to sit next to me on our driftwood seat, I'm thankful for the little fire that I've built. I find that a campfire makes it easier for people to talk about uncomfortable stuff, giving two people something to look at instead of right in the eyes, which can be disconcerting. That's especially true for me.

"So. My father owes money to loan sharks. Loan sharks who work for some nasty guys, who in turn answer to one of the bigger drug kingpins in the state of California. I figured it out pretty quickly one night at my thirteenth birthday party. My father was never that attentive to my day-to-day needs; I was mostly raised by nannies. But whenever my birthday rolled around, he made a huge show of it. Professional entertainment, party planners, A-list guest list. The works. I didn't care; I just wanted to hang out with my friends. When I turned thirteen, some strange men showed up to the house and, right in front of everyone, took all the pretty boxes from the gift table and casually loaded them in their car. When I asked my dad what was going on, he pretended it was a joke. He was terrible at covering his ass. So I walked right up to one of the big, burly men and asked them. They all ignored me except one. He just turned to me, kneeled, and gently said, 'You tell your daddy, this is what happens the first time he doesn't pay his bills.'

"From then on, I knew I was more or less on my own. My nanny helped me film my fashion and makeup tutorials, and I started my channel. Still, my whole life has been lived in the shadow of these scary men, always on the perimeter. Dad hired a bodyguard and acted like that made him Super Dad.

"Then last year, my father brought me into the conference room at his studio, where a scary-looking man informed me that I was going to marry his son in six months, or my father was going to lose everything. The drug cartel was going to take his studio, which was making a decent income by that time, away from him. Instead, my father worked out a deal. I would marry the kingpin's son, Louie, who's a big deal in his own right. Art fraud, weapons smuggling, all kinds of shady shit. I wasn't interested. But I could see they were serious. And I knew my father would never give up that studio to save me; he'd always be protecting his ass first. So instead of saying no, I took the path of least resistance. These men were terrifying. I knew that even if they took everything away from my father, that they'd never leave me alone. So I said yes, and insisted on planning the whole thing: the wedding, the honeymoon, everything. My instincts were correct; I was mostly left to my own devices by making a big show of how much I enjoyed all that work.

"So, when Sierra told me she wanted to have a baby on her own and wanted to do it outside of the scrutiny of her own unimpressive family, I hatched the plan. I made arrangements to get the hell out of the U.S. earlier than planned. And we used the honeymoon package I'd booked with Louie's money for ourselves. And that's how I ended up a runaway bride."

So many things happen inside me all at once. Gratitude that she confided all this to me. Shock at this unbelievable story. And an overwhelming need to never let her leave my sight ever again.

And, finally, the need to tell her the truth.

Chapter Eight

Jax

I WAIT for the inevitable bad reaction. Disbelief. Revulsion. Terror. A distancing away from me out of self-preservation.

But Brooks doesn't do any of that.

He simply asks, "Are you safe now?"

This simple question—these four small words—speak volumes more than any time in my life that I've ever heard anyone tell me they love me. Other than Sierra and my nannies, I've rarely felt believed, understood, and seen. And then the stupid tears well up, and I have to will them away.

My voice cracking, I answer, "For the first time in my life, I'm not being watched—either by bodyguards or by people who need something from me—and this is the first time I feel like I'm in complete control. Safe? Maybe, maybe not. In control of my life? Yeah, which is better." I look up from the fire and study Brooks's face. If he doesn't kiss me or hug me now, I don't know what I'll do. Maybe he needs a signal from me.

"Can I hug you now?" I ask.

To my shock and disappointment, he holds up his hands. "Wait. Before you decide you want me to touch you, it's my turn to tell you something."

Oh, no. I knew he was too good to be true. He's going to tell me something creepy. I've been secretly hoping he's a quiet geek with an affinity for crazy jungle sex, but maybe he's been silent all this time for other reasons. Is he married? Separated? Wanted in the U.S. for tax fraud? Of course? Why else do people expatriate to a rock in the middle of the ocean? Unless…oh god…it's something much, much worse.

But I look into Brooks's eyes, and I know. He could not hurt anyone, not even if he wanted to.

"Here it is," he says, finally, taking a deep breath. "I knew who you were the second I laid eyes on you."

I sigh in relief. "You're a follower of mine. It's not weird; I just wish you'd let me know earlier."

Brooks drags his hand over his face. "You don't get what I'm saying. Let me explain."

He then tells me about how he fell for me at the tender young age of 13. I'm grateful he leaves out the most personal "after-school-special" details of how exactly I became imprinted on his young brain. Which is more than I can say for a lot of men on the internet.

It's all rather sweet and feels like…well, there's no other word for it. "Kismet."

With a furrowed brow, he repeats the word. "Kismet."

"Yeah!" I nudge him with my foot. "We were meant to meet each other."

"Meant to…?"

"Destiny."

Brooks looks skeptical, then smiles. "Happy coincidence."

"Call it whatever you want. It's pretty incredible."

He lifts one shoulder. "I believe in science, so I'll call it an accident."

"Well, I believe it science too, but an accident? That's a bleak word."

"A nice accident. A happy accident."

"That sounds like I peed my pants, and it turned to rainbow glitter."

Brooks laughs, and though I'm glad he finds me funny, I wonder when he's going to kiss me.

"I'm not good at this, so I'm just going to say it. Can I hold your hand?"

Brightly, only half-joking, I nod and ask, "Against what would you like to hold it?"

Too far? Probably. But I'm trying to poke the beast awake again.

When he shows me no reaction, I find myself begin a massive apology for all the sex jokes.

Brooks leans over and, while I'm in the middle of speaking, silences me with a kiss on my cheek, then on the other cheek, and then my lips. I capture his lips in mine, and all the words I had started to say float away. I'm so full of thoughts I don't know where to start most of the time. But in the middle of this kiss, in the middle of paradise, I have no thoughts.

The kiss only lasts a few seconds, but they are the warmest, sweetest, and most present seconds of my life.

I want him to do it again, as soon as possible.

When his alarm rings on his phone, I'm reminded that he's an employee here and I'm a guest. He has work to do. Appointments to keep.

"Better head back," he says. "When can I see you again?"

"Come out with Sierra and me tonight."

He hesitates, then says, "I don't do great at nightclubs. Too many people, too loud."

"You prefer the company of tortoises and sharks, don't you, Brooks?"

Brooks brushes the hair from my face and says, "I want to do this right. I have some free time tomorrow before one of my tours. Let me take you for a boat ride to one of my favorite spots."

Honestly, I don't care where he takes me. We could be on the moon as long as he keeps kissing me. Being courted is lovely, romantic, and ideal in the everyday world. This is not what I expected on vacation. Isn't the age-old story that a person engages in a hot vacation fling and returns home a little heartbroken after catching feelings? But look at him, taking care of me. Feeding me. Entertaining me. Showing me unique places I'd never get to see otherwise.

On top of that, he doesn't kiss like someone who's having a flirtation or a fling, like a man who'll kiss anybody. His tongue slides and teases as if it already knows the terrain, knows how to get me going. He heightens my bliss and keeps me there. Brooks says he's not good at dating, but that's what he's doing. And dating is not a thing we have time for with the days I have left here.

And, what if he's the kind of guy who wants to romance me and wait until my last night on the island to have sex? Would that be so terrible?

A small part of me says, yes. *Kick it up a notch. Let's do this; we're on the clock.*

And then, another part of me, the one that wants the fantasy despite knowing it's not possible, says, *Time is a construct. Just let it be.*

Chapter Nine

Brooks

"Looks like I'll getting some tail this week. That Instagram chick signed up for every last one of my events this week."

I freeze, and my ears perk up. "Who?"

I've stopped inside the resort administrative offices to pick up my paycheck and place an order for a fresh supply of coral-safe sunscreen. Baker, the water sports director, is checking the schedule on a large whiteboard. He twirls the keys to the speedboat on the first knuckle of his middle finger, a predatory look on his face. "That influencer chick with the hot ass."

I don't want to jump to conclusions, especially when I already am biased — for a good reason — against Baker. He's got zero boundaries with guests. I should not be surprised he's talking about anybody in this rude manner. And also, my attitude is always on edge whenever I have to

do things in this office with its fluorescent lighting and…
well…walls.

"Are you talking about Jax Pierce?"

Baker looks over the spreadsheet on the computer in front of him. "Yeah, that's her. I don't know what she's into, but we're going to get to know each other pretty well."

Several things occur to me at the moment. One: if Jax has signed up for every damn outing on this island, including mine and Baker's, then she does not want to sit still for long. This means, if I let my imagination run wild, she's running from something. She is either not safe from her ex-fiance Louie, or she doesn't feel safe. Either way, that's not acceptable to me, and I will have to figure out how to handle this situation. Or, she wants to pack in every adventure she can while visiting the islands, and maybe I need to cool my jets.

"What's the matter with you?" Baker asks.

I realize I'm not doing a great job of concealing my irritation.

"Nothing," I say, a little too abruptly.

Baker laughs and says, "Buddy, don't bother. You're not her type. She's a wild one."

He shows me his phone screen, which plays a video of Jax and her friend dancing, nearly naked, definitely drunk at the Mumbling Ahab. At one point in the video, her bikini top falls, exposing a nipple. Howling with laughter, she quickly covers up again and keeps dancing.

There's nothing that shocking about this scene; resort guests do this sort of thing all the time. There's even a bar somewhere on the islands that offers free drinks to women who lift their tops. What's curious to me is why Baker filmed it.

My blood now boiling, I seethe, "Delete that video."

"Come on, man. I'm sure her followers would love to see what she gets up to on vacation."

All I can think of is what she told me about her family, how they don't know where she is. A video posted like that will give her away and put her in real danger.

"You know as well as I do that one of the rules is we don't take embarrassing videos of guests."

"Dude, I'm not going to post it. But I'm sure one of her rival TikTokers would pay good money to embarrass her."

Without thinking twice, I rip the phone out of his hands and delete the video myself.

"What the fuck are you doing, Eagle Scout?!"

I stuff his phone in my pocket and hold out my hand. "And now you're going to give me the keys to the speedboat if you want your phone back." For the record, I do not recognize this man I've turned into this morning. Everything I feel for Jax has turned me into a different person. I've never stood up to guys like Baker before. But taking his phone and telling him what he's going to do feels as automatic as breathing.

"What? Why?"

"Because I don't want you going out alone with any female guests today. Maybe not ever again."

Baker laughs. "You're not my supervisor, friend."

"No, but I do outclass your trashy ass."

He's not going to back down. His face is on the verge of laughter. "Why don't you run along to the nature center and wait for the geriatrics? That's the only way a snake is getting petted in your world, Barrow."

I step closer to him, not knowing what exactly I plan to do if this conversation devolves into fisticuffs. "If I feel like you are a danger to the guests, I can report you. So I'm giving you the option."

He sneers. "You're going to report me if I don't let you do my job today?"

Shaking my head, I reply, "No. First, I'll punch your lights out. Then I'll report you."

His attitude changes now that I'm more or less speaking a language he understands. His palms up in surrender, Baker replies, "All right, tough guy. If you want to get physical over it, then let's arm wrestle for it. Like gentlemen."

I don't know if it's the newfound beast within me, but somehow, this works.

Twenty minutes later, I'm on the dock with a probably sprained elbow and the keys to the speedboat.

I find Jax and her friend sitting side by side on the dock, Jax's tanned little foot flexed and her big toe pointed down and circling in the water. The way she looks so relaxed —the slow, circling motion in the water, her easy laughter with her friend—has me pitching a tent pole in my drawers so big and hard I could house a three-ring circus in here.

When Jax turns to me, her pleasant surprise is better than anything in this world.

"Hey!"

If this is her first gut reaction to seeing me, then I know I'm doing something right. I make it my goal in life to make her smile like that every day.

Chapter Ten

Jax

I'm so glad I signed up for parasailing, even though I'm afraid of heights. I'm even more pleased that Brooks was the one to take us out on the water this morning.

Although Sierra was unbelievably writing up a pro-con list while zipping through the water in a speedboat, I was happy she was there to see me. I am elated to watch her do what I just did; the only thing better than overcoming my fears is to watch my best friend sailing through the air.

This moment makes me so happy that I stand up in the boat, wind whipping my hair into my face, and shout to her, "We do what we want!"

I have no idea if she hears me, but Brooks is freaking out a little bit. The next thing I know, he's pulled me into his lap in the captain's chair.

I'm soaked in my wetsuit, but he doesn't seem to care. "We meet again, Dr. Jones."

"Are you ever going to stop calling me that?" Brooks

asks, raising his voice to be heard over the sound of the wind and the engine.

"Depends on how nice you are," I say.

I turn my face over my shoulder and up, awkwardly as I sit here in his lap facing forward, but still, I can see the expression on his face. That wild, heated look returns, and I feel a momentary sense of triumph.

I move to stand, but he locks his arms around me as he steers the boat. I crane around as much as I possibly can, so I can look up and wave at Sierra, who waves back. I wriggle against Brooks's arms, but I'm no match for him.

"What's your next move, nature boy?"

A thrill runs through me at the sensation of his hot breath on the shell of my ear. And, is my mind playing tricks on me, or do I feel a scrape of teeth?

Maybe things are about to kick up a notch between us. The more I wriggle against his grip, the deeper I feel a steely length push into my hip. Oh. No maybe about it.

That's when his right hand lets go of the wheel and cinches me against him. I gasp as he thrusts forward a little, making sure I know what he's thinking. I press back, gripping his hand that's around my waist and guiding it, so it rests between my thighs.

I don't think either of us will deboard this vessel without first doing some bad, bad things.

Brooks slows the engine, and his fingers dig into my thighs, flooding my core with anticipation. He rasps in my ear as he slows the boat to set Sierra back down in the water gently. "My next move? I don't have any moves. But when we get back to the dock, you're going to make up an excuse."

"I don't need an excuse. We're adults. And she's already on to us."

Brooks's hand drags up from my thigh and shocks me

by cupping my pussy over my wetsuit. I gasp, and he murmurs in my ear, "What I've got for you, my little dragonfly, is more than a crush."

My knees tremble as he lets me up and goes to help Sierra back into the boat.

She removes her wetsuit and looks at me curiously, clearly wondering why I'm still wearing mine. I unzip and toss it aside, feeling Brooks's eyes on every inch of me. The memory of his words in my ear still sends tingles down my spine; my nipples remain hard and pebbled, remembering how we were just grinding on each other right under my friend's nose. And my core will never forget that little squeeze from that big, rough hand through my wetsuit.

I try to put the anticipation of whatever he might have planned out of my head as he drives us back to the dock. Sierra and I excitedly celebrate this thrilling moment for both of us, but at the same time, I'm so excited for what happens next that I can't even look at Brooks.

The island's resident nerd has me happily in his grip.

Chapter Eleven

Brooks

I DON'T RECOGNIZE myself around Jax, but at the same time, I feel like I've found another part of myself that I've been missing my entire life: The man who knows exactly what he wants when he sees it and wants it now.

Her kiss stays with me after she's gone. I don't want to go to work after being with her, and I always want to go to work.

Kissing her again on this boat, as the waves gently sway, feels like coming home. Home to what? Myself? My girlfriend? My wife? Yes. Yes, to all of it.

Moving us to the row of seats at the bow, Jax seats herself right where I want her, her legs across my lap, and we continue kissing. Her mouth opens to my teasing tongue, her arms hug my neck, and her knees clench my hand.

"So, this is your favorite spot on the island you were telling me about?"

"Are you here, Jax?"

Through her sweet kisses, she murmurs a yes.

"Then it's my favorite."

Her laugh makes the sun in my sky shine brighter. "You're a lot more charming than you think you are."

But I know that's not the truth. I just love being with her. She owns me. Jax Pierce has owned me since I was a hopeless romantic at 13.

I don't believe in fate, but I can't deny that meeting her and living out my childhood dream seems like enough of a coincidence to make me a believer.

As our kisses and pets heat up, egged on by the gentle rocking of the boat, Jax shows me what she likes with her soft moans, sighs, and wriggles. She tastes like saltwater and exotic fruit. Her mouth opens to me more the deeper I probe with our kiss.

I'm such a hungry, careless bastard I fear I might choke her with my tongue, but she opens her throat and takes more. I groan into her mouth. My cock twitches at the suggestiveness of it. I don't expect a deep-throat, but I can just imagine those full lips wrapped around my cock, taking all of me, all the way back.

Maybe that will happen, and perhaps it won't.

All I care about right now is making sure she's having a good time.

I don't want to come up for air; all I want is to keep drinking her in. Human biology, however, dictates other-wise. "I'm not who you think I am," I say, breathless, remembering all the rules I broke to get us out here.

I was supposed to return the boat keys to Baker as soon as we had returned to the dock after parasailing. But that's not what I did.

Sierra and Jax had said their goodbyes at the dock — Sierra shooting me a warning look that implied I'd better be good to her friend — and then I threw caution to the ocean breeze. And now, here we are, around the eastern tip of the island at Pirate's Cove. Miles from the main resort and in the middle of reefs too dangerous for most watercraft to interrupt our time together.

It's not exactly guaranteed to be private, but I've discovered my rebellious streak, and I'm going with it.

With one more precious kiss from her lips, Jax pulls back and smiles, though her eyes are hooded. "I know exactly who you are. I've been doing my homework since yesterday. Isolating me in a remote cove barely accessible to rescue boats. I think you mean to ravage me, Dr. Jones."

Chapter Twelve

Jax

Before I finish that sentence, the man Brooks has me
straddling his lap, his eyes daring me to say no.

He growls. "Isn't that what you want, angel?"

I nod my head dumbly, taken aback at the strain in his
voice. He sounds as if someone or something is holding
him back on a leash, and he's just within nipping distance
of what he wants. This is such a change from yesterday.
He's the same person but hungrier. I'm one part nervous at
the ferocity lurking behind his eyes and two parts humming
with curiosity.

He cups my face and kisses me fiercely.

"There's something else you should know. The
douchebag who usually runs this boat pissed me off, and I
want to fuck you in it out of spite. It's not normal for me,
so if that turns you off, say the word."

Relieved, I nod my head again. "I'm down to be petty
with you. He must have really pissed you off, Doctor."

The husky growl from him vibrates everywhere our bodies touch. "He implied he was going to make a play for you, and I fucking lost it."

I shouldn't have these feelings about men fighting over me. I didn't think the man was capable of such coarse language. But holy shit, the nerdy doctor losing his mind with jealousy makes me slick with need.

"Some other guy sniffs around, and you need to mark your territory?" I tease.

Brooks' rough hands on my nearly bare cheeks pull me closer, though our hips already are fused. "You don't understand," he says. "You're already mine."

One half of my brain wants to challenge this whole idea; I don't belong to anyone but myself. The other half says: *Yes, Nature Boy. I'm yours.*

"Convince me. Make me yours, then," I say.

Brooks's mouth owns mine in a kiss so intense I forget where I am. His hands drag down my back, down my legs, around the cheeks of my ass, up my sides. My body tracks the path of his hands everywhere, the steady, low groans promising to unleash a beast on me. I'm ready for it.

I feel his inner conflict as we kiss and pet, grope, and struggle with buttons, strings, and zippers. He wants to go slow, he wants me to enjoy it, but he has a need. A deep, deep hunger of someone who's been starved of affection for so long and is so close to getting what he wants he could explode at any moment.

His fingers pull my bikini bottom aside, and he wets one digit between my folds. A gasp escapes me, followed by a moan when that finger nudges around my clit, exploring every inch of my most sensitive skin. He curses softly into my mouth. "You're so fucking wet; is that for me, my little dragonfly?"

My thoughts have melted into the moment, and all I

can think about is saying "yes." Yes to his kisses, yes to his hands lightly teasing up and down my spine, yes to the slow torment of one finger, then a second, sinking into my core.

His free hand works loose the hook at the back of my top, and I arch back from him to slide it off my shoulders, letting the wet fabric fall to the floor of the boat with a slap.

Brooks draws a whimper out of me when he pulls away from my pussy so he can cup both my breasts. "Beautiful," he says, gently squeezing, tenderly kissing. Watching his expression as his thumbs tease my nipples into tight peaks sends a fresh wave of need through me. He nuzzles, kisses, teases at first, then latches on. He keeps up the gentle squeezing while his teeth and tongue play, nip and suck.

For the first time with a partner, I come. I never thought any man could get me there. A watery cry of surprise ends in complete, blissed-out gibberish.

Imagine a guy being able to make a girl come by the strength of pure enthusiasm and awe. How? How did he do that?

Brooks sees what's happening and grips me close, kissing me through it, forcing me to moan into his mouth. He pulls back, and I gasp at the surprise sensation of his hands on my rump, spreading me open.

I reach down into his unzipped fly and let Brooks see my cheeks blush as I pull out his length. My eyes cut down to get a look at it. Dark pink and veiny, his thick, warm cock pulsates in my hands.

The sea breeze cools my wet skin, and I involuntarily shiver. Brooks notices this, of course. "Oh shit. I'm such a rude asshole. Your cold."

"Don't say that," I say, smoothing my hand over his length, teasing his ridge, noticing the bead of precum at the tip. I lick my lips. "That's why I brought a towel."

I slide off of him and carefully grab the beach towel from the back of the boat, wrapping it around my shoulders. I fully intend to hurry back to the bow, but when I try to turn around, he's right behind me in the stern. Pressed up against me, his hands float around to my stomach, holding me still as we both struggle to stand against the rocking.

"What are you doing, Brooks?"

He teases the shell of my ear with his tongue and teeth, the nudge of his cock against my bare ass triggering a fresh ache between my legs. "I couldn't stand being away from you for a second."

Not for one measly second while I'm fetching a towel? *It's okay, Jax, just go with how good that makes you feel.*

"We'd better sit down before we fall," I rasp, the first logical thought I've had in minutes.

Grunting, "Fine," Brooks agrees and takes a seat in the stern of the speedboat.

"Don't be surly. I have a present for you," I say.

Placing both hands on his thighs, I settle down on my knees in front of him, taking his cock in my hands once more, watching Brooks's face flood with heat.

He rasps, "Jax, wait. Wait, we have company."

That's when I hear the sound of jet skis in the distance. I peek up over the side and see a pair of them buzzing around the horn of the island, heading toward the cove where we are.

"Fuck," Brooks mutters.

I look up at him and grin. "No reason to let anyone else ruin our fun."

Shocked, he stumbles over some words about being in public.

I shrug and tell him, "Once again, towels have many uses."

Chapter Thirteen

Brooks

I SHOULD NOT ALLOW THIS. I should stop this right now. I should protect her dignity at all costs.

But no matter how many ways I scold myself, the more I know I'm going to let it happen.

Let her slide that towel over her head, rest her elbows on my thighs, and go to town on me.

At the first touch of her damp lips to the top of my cock, my body twitches. "Ah…Jax…oh god, there's something you should know."

Her head remains under the towel. I first think she's just blatantly ignoring me, but I hear and feel her question—"Hmm?"—vibrate, her breath wafting over my skin and her tongue—holy fuck that sweet pink tongue—licking off my precum.

"Fuck." Breathe, Brooks. Breathe.

"No one's ever done this to me before. I'm not sure what—"

Jax's head pops out from under the towel, and she smiles. "You don't need to do anything, but if you want to do something with your hands, you can pull my hair."

"I don't want to hurt you," I breathe.

The jet skis are approaching. I know she can hear them. She doesn't care. I find this whole scenario so exhilarating, I'm going to have to marry this woman.

"You won't hurt me as long as you have a nice big handful. Just push and pull if you want me to go faster or slower. Or don't…and lie back and think of the baby turtles."

The jet skis hum across the water, but my mind tunes it all out with the humming, licking, and sucking going on below this *Little Mermaid* beach towel. My lips part as I look down at the wide-eyed Disney character, whose face gets distorted as Jax's head begins to bob up and down with her stroking mouth.

So glad now I never watched a single Disney princess movie because this right here would ruin it with new perverted associations.

Jax knows how to pull me out of my head at the right moment; her hand moves from my thighs to my balls. *What…what is happening…* "Oh my god."

Fuck pulling her hair; I'm locked onto the cleat along the side of the boat. I'm working hard not to lose it as I feel her sweet, warm mouth tenderly suck, stroke, and massage my balls.

I used to think most women found blowjobs degrading, but Jax is going after it. She's annihilating any inhibitions and preconceived notions I ever had about—everything, so much so I have no idea where the jet skiers have gone, and I no longer care.

She switches, taking my length back into her mouth, cupping my balls with her hands, and gentle squeezing.

My brain is officially fried now. Everything is a haze of pink pleasure and white-hot torture combined.

She increases her pace, and I feel the tip hitting the back of her throat.

Through gritted teeth, I rumble, "My Jax. You're mine. Do you see what you do to me? Is that proof enough?"

I'm going to come, so hard. But I want—I need something more. I just need to do things I didn't want to do before and snake my hands under the towel, filling my hands with her hair. I can feel her moan against my skin as I tug her up and down. Her hands drag down to my thighs, and her nails dig in. I suck in my breath at the delightful pain of it.

"Mine," I say to her, to myself, to the whole fucking world. Jax Pierce is mine.

Cum jets down her throat. She swallows, squeezing my balls like she's trying to will them to make more. "*Fuck. Fuck. Fuuck.*" I sound like every asshole I ever heard having sex in my college freshman dorm. A doctorate in biology, and I've got no words at the moment.

Jax seems unfazed and unsurprised at my reactions.

Keeping her wrapped up in the towel, I seat her across my lap and kiss her sweet, giving mouth, caress her face, smooth the wet hair from her face.

I want this moment to last forever. I never want to stop talking to her, listening to her talk, watching her walk around like she knows she's beautiful. And why shouldn't she? Everyone should.

My heart is whole; I nearly blurt out, "I love you."

And I might feel it. It could be true.

But when I say it, the last thing I want is for Jax to believe I'm in love with her for giving me a blowjob on Baker's boat.

Breathless and smiling, she tells me, "Anytime you want

to spite one of your colleagues, just let me know. I will fly across the globe to do that again."

And that's just the problem. I can't let her do that. I can't live with the idea of Jax residing on the other side of the world, apart from me.

I need her in my life—every day.

So now, I have some thinking to do.

Chapter Fourteen

Jax

"What does one wear to a foraging tour?"

When Sierra doesn't answer her text right away, I follow up with:

"More importantly, what is foraging, and will I be expected to eat bugs?"

I'm staring at the clothes I packed and settle on some spandex athletic pants for stretch, in case there's any climbing I have to do. My camo sports bra looks pretty hot with it, but I wonder if that's too risqué, in case another family group has signed up for this.

God, I hope not. With Brooks's luck, that Isaac kid will climb trees and throw rocks at monkeys or some other horrifying behavior.

I throw a tank top over my shirt, and finally, Sierra texts me back.

"Brooks won't ask you to eat bugs."

"How do you know?"

"Are you in our room?"

I don't know what's up with that non sequitur. "Yeah, I'm about to grab a bite to eat and then meet Brooks. Why?"

"Because Austin and I need the room."

The gasp that comes out of me is heard in the hallway. I know this because she tells me so, as she's right outside the door. Instead, the two of them, Sierra and Austin, are right outside the door.

I open the door to see my best friend looking flushed and Austin looking very pleased with himself.

Rearing back, I explain, "Looks like you two already took care of hotel-room business!"

Sierra playfully swats my arm then pushes me out of the room. "Thanks, I love you, bye!"

I pout at the door and mutter that I love her too. My attitude swiftly changes when I recall that I was the one who encouraged her to loosen up to the idea of meeting someone on this trip.

Except now I have a problem: I forgot to grab my bug spray.

Knocking gently on the door, I don't expect it to open again. Mainly because I'm pretty sure Sierra and Austin are making out up against the door: I hear moaning and kissing and fabric rustling.

To my surprise, the door opens, and Sierra's hand pops out, dropping my bottle of bug spray in my hand.

"Thanks, mama," I chirp and head off to my version of a hot jungle date.

Chapter Fifteen

Brooks

WE MOVE THROUGH THE WOODS, gradually uphill as the trail hugs the side of the mountain. So far, we've gathered enough greens and mushrooms for a decent lunch. Protein seems to be out of the question, as I'm not going to push Jax to try grubs.

The long hike is sweaty, but Jax doesn't complain once. She only asks once what to do if we're confronted by wildlife, but I assure her the predatory jungle cats are no danger to us.

To take her mind off the unfamiliar, shadowy place while we gather our lunch, we share anecdotes from our childhood. I tell her I've always been fascinated by bugs, birds, and trees and even staged a protest in high school biology when they expected us to dissect a frog.

"They labeled me a wuss, and I never lived it down all through high school."

"Eh, fuck those people. My high school wouldn't let me opt out of dissecting a fetal pig, so I got an F. I refused to do it. I thought it was so horrible I didn't care if I failed."

The tone in her voice touches me. I look over and see that she and I are a lot more alike than I first thought.

Stopping on the trail, I turn and cup Jax's face in my hands. "I know it's too hot for touching, but I want to do this."

She leans in just enough to meet me as my lips capture hers. I don't care how hot and humid it is in the forest; I could stay here and kiss her like this all day.

Jax has a kiss that can compel me to ask her to marry me this minute. I don't want to say that. Who says that after knowing her only a few days? And I don't know how to work it into a conversation. Breezy is not in my nature.

I only tell her as much truth as I think she can handle at the moment. "Jax. Do you know why I call you a dragonfly?"

She smirks. "Because you think they're pretty?"

I reply, "They're a sign of a balanced ecosystem. That's what you are to me. Everything felt out of sync until I met you. Now that you're here, I feel like I have my equilibrium. I know it sounds insane, but that's how I feel. And I don't want you to leave."

Jax blushes and smiles. "I'm your dragonfly?"

"Yes, and I hate it that you're leaving next week. Everything is going to feel wrong again."

She lifts one shoulder to match her sassy little eyebrow. "Maybe I won't ever leave. It's pretty nice here."

I'm going in. "Stay with me."

The gentle press of her pelvis against mine edges me further to the brink. She's thinking, considering. I watch her face move through ten different emotions.

I won't move a muscle until she tells me what I need to hear.

I watch her throat bob up and down as she thinks, possibly swallowing some feeling she's not ready for.

Well, she'd better get ready.

Chapter Sixteen

Jax

Hearing someone say the words, "Stay with me," feels as good or better than any "I love you."

"I love you" is a special moment, an outpouring. But typically, those words are not spoken out loud until a person knows they're safe to say them.

"Stay with me" feels much more raw, vulnerable, and direct. It's a specific request. I am needed. I am wanted. He wants me to do something that's just not done: never return home from vacation, to be with him. With Brooks, it's also a promise of protection. He knows what's waiting for me back home. If I stay, I'll be putting my trust in someone who, just a few days ago, was a stranger.

I can't believe I'm thinking this over. But why not? What do I have to go back to? Guaranteed, the only person who will be speaking to me when I go back to LA is Sierra, and there's a chance she might not go back ever.

She plans to have her baby on the big island and recuperate there as well. After that, who knows.

And then, like puzzle pieces, it all comes together.

Of course. Sierra's laying low from her unsupportive family. I should be staying here to support her, at least until she's settled with the baby. Maybe even longer. Hell, I have enough squirreled away I could stay and rent a small apartment and get a job, provided I can navigate the work visa situation.

Finally, I decide. I'm jumping in with both feet. "I'll stay. Sierra's going to have her baby here; you're here. Let's try it and see what happens."

Brooks looks as if he wants to say something important. My stomach somersaults as I wait for him to speak, but then the moment passes. Instead, he speaks to me with his touch. He scoops me up into his arms and kisses me until I'm breathless. His soft yet demanding lips make my spine tremble. His kiss leaps from passionate to hungry to starving, and soon my feet leave the ground.

I don't know how he can hold me like this, but he shows no signs of strain other than the soft grunts that escape his throat with the friction where our pelvises meet.

Do I think this man intends to love me forever? As of now, he does. And now is all I have.

Chapter Seventeen

Brooks

THE KISSING HAS ESCALATED to heavy petting, to the tugging and removing of shirts. I know. Nature takes control so rapidly when humans stop talking.

I feel a dozen pairs of undomesticated animals' eyes in the shadows of the trees and undergrowth surrounding us, watching us. And I don't care. Let them watch.

"I need to taste you, sweetheart."

Neither missing a beat nor wasting a single second asking if we're too exposed, my Jax reacts enthusiastically.

Perched on the rocks at the edge of a nearby stream, Jax helps me slide her spandex pants down and off. With her lovely backside resting on my sweaty khaki shirt, I spread her open as we kiss, my greedy fingers petting her soft, sensitive skin until her moans turn urgent and my digits are coated with her slickness.

I can't resist teasing along with my strokes. I caress her with soft kisses down her neck, along her collarbone. "So soft, wet, and naughty." The goosebumps rise across her flesh while her folds drench my hand and my sweaty shirt on which she sits. *I'm never washing that shirt again.*

Finally, it's time to take what I want—all of her.

My face buries into her heat, slowly at first, then hungrily. I want to enjoy every single second with her because, as she's said, she has no idea what will happen tomorrow.

My tongue finds its home inside her warm, wet core, fitting around me so snug and cozy. She's perfect and ready for me. She tastes like the sweetest fruit, and I never want to stop.

Our first time together was a nearly public exhibition on the boat, and now it feels like a celebration. I'm fervent; I'm so overcome with joy and deep, deep need to care for her, cover her in my protection, be close to her, know everything about her…is this love? I don't know. I suppose love will show itself when it's ready.

And if she loves me back or not, everything will be alright in the end.

Everything will play out exactly as it is meant to, without too much intervention on the intellectual side of things. I've lived too much inside my head.

With her honey on my lips, dripping down my chin, I finally feel like I've let go. I lick, suck, taste, and tease, her moans and cries growing ever louder as her pelvis bucks upward.

I keep going, savoring her juices, triggering another gush with my attentions to her clit, her heated, tight cunt.

With her fingers woven through my hair, my Jax comes apart, flooding me with her sweetness, pulsating, thrusting, both of us sweaty and not caring what dangers lurk in the dark jungle.

Whatever happens, it doesn't matter. I'm here, and I'll always be the one to take care of her.

I share her taste with her, kissing her and stroking her trembling body through a long bout of aftershocks. I could keep going. I knew she'd be sweet, but holy shit, is that not the right word for it. Miraculous would be closer to what it's like having her taste slide down my throat.

When I help her ease back into her clothes and help her stand, she stumbles and falls against me, laughing. "I change my mind. That, that is what I will fly halfway around the globe for."

We laugh and seal the moment with a kiss, unaware of anyone or anything that might be watching us nearby.

If we'd been paying attention, I might have heard a branch snap or a footfall and been able to hide. Unfortunately, the danger is right on top of us by the time I realize it's there.

"The only place she's going is back to Los Angeles with me."

Chapter Eighteen

Jax

My father is not the person who stands about thirty feet away. Neither is it Louie.

The man standing about thirty feet away is Damian, my dad's most trusted confidant, the one he has entrusted to be in charge of me since I was a child, to keep predators away.

A cold, disinterested voice drawls from the phone at the man's hip. "Do you have her, Damian?"

With his eyes trained on his captor, Damian takes the phone out of the belt clip and speaks into it. "Caught her and her boyfriend trying to disappear in the forest."

His other hand rests on the butt of a sidearm on his other hip.

"Damian. Come on. A runaway bride is hardly worth this much effort," I say. "I know my dad isn't paying you enough to travel this far."

He shrugs, taking the gun out of the holster. "That's correct. Fortunately, other people see my worth."

The cold voice on the other end of the phone speaks again. "Good. We'll have a boat waiting for you at the dock to bring her back to the yacht."

I should be feeling terrified right now, shouldn't I? After all, I ran away rather than stand my ground, and now they've found me. But I feel nothing but calm and focus. A few days ago, I lost my balance over a harmless basking shark. Today, I'm watching a man I've known most of my life lift a gun and aim it at me, and I feel … nothing. As if that man belongs to a chapter in the last book I read, trying to elbow his way into the book I'm currently reading. He doesn't belong here.

Brooks—my darling, daring, brave, and very stupid man—has placed himself in the middle. I wish I could signal to him not to worry. Damian is not going to shoot anyone if I don't go with him. "She's not going anywhere with you."

Damian chuckles. "But our girl is such a compliant little sweetheart. Sure she'll come back. She just got a little spooked, but everything will be right as rain."

I bristle. "Don't call me that. I'm not your sweetheart. You're nothing to me."

Brooks reaches behind his back, and I instinctively grab his hand.

"I've been there for you, Jax," Damian said. "I've always had your back. Your father trusted me always to know where you were. And then you pull this crap."

Keep him talking, Jax. "When are you and my father going to realize I'm a grown woman? I don't need your protection anymore."

Damian isn't finished letting me have it. "I always did everything I was asked to do. I kept you away from dangerous men. I kept you safe all these years, and this is how you thank me? Do you want me to lose everything?"

I spit out, "You say that, but you didn't protect me from the real threat. You didn't try to stop my father from marrying me off to that slug of a human being. If you cared about me at all, you would have helped me get away."

Damian replies, "I don't think you get it. I came here to make sure you were okay and to make sure your father doesn't die as a result of your actions."

"Die?" I'm confused. "They said they would take his business. That's all."

"Your father fired me on the spot when you flew the coop, Jax. Louie was so livid he's now keeping your dad hostage until you come home. Yeah, these guys are not known for sticking to the terms of their agreements. So Louie hired me to track you down, and he's waiting offshore, right now."

Chapter Nineteen

Brooks

I don't quite understand all the moving pieces here.

But I do understand two things. One, Jax belongs to me now, and no thug with a gun is taking her anywhere. Two, I have one strategy in my arsenal: I know this forest like the back of my hand.

Fortunately, the man with the gun doesn't know where we are relative to the hotel; I can tell by the way he's glancing around, looking for the trail. The untrained eye wouldn't be able to see it.

So I make an offer and pray he takes it.

"Fine," I say. "I'll get you both back to the hotel."

"What?" Jax squeaks.

My hand squeezes hers tightly, hoping she understands. I have a plan. Well, an idea. A nugget of an idea. All right, a half-assed shaving from a chunk of an idea.

After some negotiations and convincing, the three of us

trudge through the jungle, but we're not headed back to the hotel.

There are only two ways out of this jungle. Hiking is my preferred method. There's only one other person on this rock who knows this terrain as well as I do and who knows how to get in and out quickly. Fortunately, that person also happens to be romantically attached to Jax's partner in crime.

When Jax, Damian, and I arrive at a spot where I know we can get a signal, I make my move.

"I gotta go up there to get my bearings," I say, pointing to a giant boulder jutting out of the earth, guessing that Damian won't want to follow me based on his hiking prowess thus far.

"No funny business," he orders.

Noticing Damian's level of tiredness, I take a risk. "Just going to check my phone's compass." That's my very flimsy cover story while firing off a text. But I don't think this guy is a stone-cold killer. He looks like he would rather be home with his grandchildren than trudging through the jungle.

I stuff my phone back into my shorts and climb back down. Jax gives me a tight smile, and I have to fight every instinct in my body to scoop her up and carry her off. If there were no guns, we'd fight each other like men. Baker might be a douche, but when he agreed to arm-wrestle me for the boat, he had more honor than this man.

Leading Jax and Damian off the established trail through challenging underbrush, I hold out hope to physically wear down our captor. I might not have a gun, but I know things. Specifically, I know of a clearing about a mile from here.

I hope this works.

Chapter Twenty

Jax

I KNOW what Brooks is doing, but I don't say it out loud.

I don't know much about hiking or jungle trails, but this is not the way back to the hotel. I trust Brooks completely, and I know this is part of a plan.

As soon as we're out of danger, I'm going to tell him I love him, and I don't even care if he says it first.

When we reach the clearing, Damian blurts out, breathless, tired, and sweating, "This is not the way we came."

Without missing a beat, Brooks replies, "Shortcut. Let's take a water break. We're going to need our energy for the rest of the trip. It's shorter but uphill."

Wow. My man is a bullshitter. Who knew?

I observe Damian as I sip my water. He looks confused and suspicious, on top of his exhaustion. Tailing me around the big city back home in an air-conditioned Suburban isn't much training for this sort of terrain. If he weren't trying to kidnap me at the moment, I might feel sorry for him.

I switch my gaze to examine Brooks. He looks nervously at me as we drink from our water bottles. Something is supposed to happen here, but I don't know what.

I do know how to take a cue. I pipe up, "I gotta pee. Be right back."

Damian perks up. "You're not going anywhere without me, missy."

Brooks might be nervous on the inside, but that doesn't stop him from standing his ground. "Until she's off this island, she's my girlfriend, and no way are you accompanying her to the little girls' room."

How much do I adore this man?

As much as I'd love to watch these two men argue, I do have to pee. Disappearing behind some trees, I drag out the time as long as I can without causing suspicion. I don't know what I'm stalling for, but it seems like Brooks is up to something, and I'm going with my gut.

The sound of a small aircraft approaches from the distance.

Then, through the treetops, Austin Fisher's little Cessna lands in the clearing, but not before very nearly clipping Damian and sending him hurtling to the ground in terror, sending his pistol sailing across the clearing. Brooks jumps him and pins him down.

Brooks shouts at me to get his pack. When I bring it to him, he's struggling on the ground with Damian, who is bigger and meaner, if not nearly as athletic as Brooks.

"Shoot him!"

I scream, "I've never shot a gun!"

"Not the pistol! In my pack!" Brooks shouts.

I look inside the pack, and I see it. He means I'm supposed to shoot Damian with a tranquilizer gun.

"Wait a minute," I say. "Why do you have this?"

"Jax."

"You said we weren't in any danger from the big kitties, so why—?"

"Jax! Not now!"

Oh. Right. Not the point.

Finally, I gather my courage and do yet one more thing on this vacation I've never done before. Shoot a man with a big-cat tranquilizer and help haul him away on a tiny plane.

Chapter Twenty-One

Jax

LOUIE DOESN'T HAVE my father killed.

Not that he wouldn't. But it turns out that my father, always the big talker, was able to convince him that he needs him around. Louie doesn't know the first thing about producing records. My father might be terrible with money, but he knows how to build money-makers.

The kingpin and his thugs most definitely did take over my father's music recording studio.

And I'm told that if I ever come back to the States, Louie will find a way to pay me back for the embarrassment of leaving him at the altar. Believe me when I say I moved all of my assets to the island with a quickness.

I may never see my father again, but he made his bed. He decided where his loyalties lay long ago.

As for me, I'm standing on the edge of a cliff, about to jump.

I look down and experience slight vertigo as I see my

toes curl at the edge of the rock. Below me is startling blue water, smooth and calm, a little jewel set apart from the crashing waves on the other side of the inlet.

I'm not afraid. I've done everything there is to do on this island, except this one thing.

I'm not afraid of anything anymore.

A man's hand slips into mine.

I look next to me, and Brooks is there. I have a good feeling he'll always be there. "Ready?"

"You're going to do this with me?"

"I'm going to do everything with you. I'll hold your hand when you jump off a cliff, whatever kind of cliff."

"I love you," I breathe.

He smiles. "I know."

"That's Han Solo, not Dr. Jones," I tease.

"Dr. Jones never settled down. Han Solo is a more loyal character."

I shake my head. "I love you, nerd. Let's go."

I suck in my breath and bend my knees, getting ready to fling myself off the rock.

"I love you too, my dragonfly."

Epilogue

One year later

Jax

THE NATURE NERDS is not something I ever thought I would hear used about me.

My and Brooks's social media following has exploded with a shared channel devoted to exploration and environmental awareness.

Brooks and I still work together at Cerulean Resort, but we travel around the world together in the off-season, giving talks and filming our adventures.

Sierra teases me about turning into a bug nerd. Honestly, I'm still squeamish around bugs and wildlife, but as long as Brooks is with me, I'm in good hands.

Even after a whole year together, he still likes to sit with me and kiss me as the sun sets. On this particular night, I've got unsettling news.

Brooks is poring over his planner for the following year and bouncing ideas off me. "We could do Bali and then Australia, or we could do South Korea first and work our way down and across Oceania before we come back home. Or we could cancel all of it and do a tour of southern Africa. I know you've always wanted to surf in South Africa, so I'll book lessons for you."

I rest my hand on his forearm.

"I think we'll be staying home all next year," I say.

He doesn't hear me at first, or perhaps he's tuning me out. "We could also do China since we've never been there. They have this crazy arachnid I've been dying to see in person at the zoo there…wait. What did you say?" Brooks turns to me and blinks.

I smile and sip my soda. "I said all next year is canceled, I think."

"Why? What's wrong? Are you sick? Did something happen? Do you not like it anymore? I know I said that if you ever decide you don't want to do this anymore, we could stop, no questions asked, but I'm sorry, I have questions."

I place my index finger over his lips to gently silence him. He's ready to move heaven and earth on a whim, just for me, at a moment's notice. I love him so damn much.

"I'm not sick. But the doctor says it's best if I don't travel anywhere too remote."

His brows come together. "Why?"

"Because although I may be acclimated to island life, I'm still a city girl at heart. And, I'd like to deliver at a hospital here or at least somewhere with an actual hospital and a NICU, just in case."

Brooks's jaw drops, and he stares at me with a look of such incredulity I think I've shorted out his brain.

"I've missed a few pieces here. Baby, are you pregnant?"

"As of three weeks ago? Yes."

I can see his brain doing the math. "Three weeks ago…" he mutters, tapping his lip.

"That's when we were on Temple Island, drunk on fermented mangos…." I remind him.

He laughs. "Oh yeah. Me, you and the monkeys."

"Fortunately, the monkeys left us alone."

"But they didn't take too kindly to us using their sturdiest branch." We do have a shared affinity for outdoor shenanigans.

I stare at him and wait for him to absorb what's happening.

Without another word, and as calm as can be, my Brooks slides his hand over my tummy. "We're going to have a little bug? All to ourselves?"

I laugh and dryly say, "No, we have to sacrifice it to the volcano god," I say. Thank god I settled down with a man who appreciates my weird sense of humor.

His eyes brighten, and he says, "We should have the baby in the volcano."

"No."

"We could set up a glamping tent; it'll be as cozy as our house."

"No, Brooks."

"The resort employs a doula," he offers.

"Brooks, I swear to god…."

Brooks catches my lip between his, and all thoughts of continuing this ridiculous argument evaporate.

"I love you, my little dragonfly," he whispers.

"You're going to be the best daddy ever," I say.

"As long as the kid likes the outdoors, otherwise I'm not sure what to do."

I think for a moment and remind him of the time he almost lost a kid on the volcano tour. "Well, if he turns out to be a brat, we can always push him down into the crater," I say.

"Hopefully, by that time, he'll already know how to swim," Brooks replies.

"He's ours; of course he will."

We sit and share a comfortable silence as the sun goes down. Waiting for the arrival of our next chapter, and excited to see what the dawn brings.

My person. My people. My family. Myself. We are all where we need to be. I didn't need to learn to stop running away; I just needed to run to the right place.

THE END

THANK you for reading Honeymoon Hideout! If you enjoyed this short story, don't forget to check out Babymoon for Sierra and Austin's story!

Please visit my website at authorabbyknox.com for links to more titles to read, and to follow me on all social media. While you're there, don't forget to sign up for my newsletter to keep up with the latest releases and announcements!

About the Author

Abby Knox writes feel-good, high-heat romance that she herself would want to read. Readers have described her stories as quirky, sexy, adorable, and hilarious. All of that adds up to Abby's overall goal in life: to be kind and to have fun!

Abby's favorite tropes include: Forced proximity, opposites attract, grumpy/sunshine, age gap, boss/employee, fated mates/insta-love, and more. Abby is heavily influenced by Buffy the Vampire Slayer, Gilmore Girls, and LOST. But don't worry, she won't ever make you suffer like Luke & Lorelai.

If any or all of that connects with you, then you came to the right place.